I Give You My Love

Compiled by John Stevenson
Designed by Anne Marie Trechslin

You saw something in me
that no one else did...
When I was lonely,
you made me feel
like I belonged,
when I was uncertain,
you helped me see things
more clearly.
And you never gave up on me,
even when I was ready
to give up on myself.
Everything is so much better
for me now...

because you saw something special in me.

$\mathcal{I}$ used to wonder when
I fell in love with you,
and I could never really pin it down
to a day or an hour or even a moment.
I've learned since then
that I never really
fell in love with you at all—
we met, we talked,
we shared, and then,
we grew in love.
And the nicest part of it all
is that we always will.

Knowing You
Makes All the Difference

Knowing you'll be there
with a hug and a smile
when things go wrong
makes all the difference.

Knowing you'll be there
to share in my joy
when life is good
makes all the difference.

And, as days pass
and seasons change,
knowing I can count
on your love and support
will always make
all the difference to me.

I love looking back
to where we began,
seeing us as we were
at the beginning,
then slowly leafing through
the memories
we've made together
to bring us
to where we are today.

I love anticipating
the days ahead of us,
wondering what we'll find
in each other,
in ourselves,
before another year
has slipped away.

But, best of all,
I love being with you
where we are today,
together writing the pages
we'll remember tomorrow.

From the very beginning,
we've known it was right for us
to be "us."
As time passed
we saw our love grow stronger,
deeper, truer,
making each of us
a better person today
and making the thought of
"us" tomorrow
a promise of all the love
we'll continue to find
in each other.

Today...
tomorrow...
always...
I love you.

The world has always held
beautiful things,
but with you
I see them more clearly.
The world has always held wonder,
but with you
I feel it more deeply.
In sharing my life with you,
the world is more exciting, more alive.

You have opened my eyes
to beauty and joy,
and I open my heart
to thank you with these words —
I love you.

Our Love
Always Makes It Work

Every relationship
has its uncertainties,
and ours is no different.
But what is different about us
is that we've worked through the doubts
and have overcome them,
because we know that being together
means being understanding
and forgiving.

In some ways,
I'm glad for the uncertainties,
because they've strengthened us both
and have taught us
the greatest lesson of all:
we need each other,
today and forever.

I often tell you I love you
and say how glad I am
we found each other,
talk about how much
you mean to me,
and how wonderful life is
because of you,
but I don't recall
ever saying "thank you" –
for liking me
and accepting me as I am,
for loving me
and letting me know it,
and for sharing with me
in your own special way...

But in my heart,
I thank you all the time,
for lots of things —
most of all, for being you.

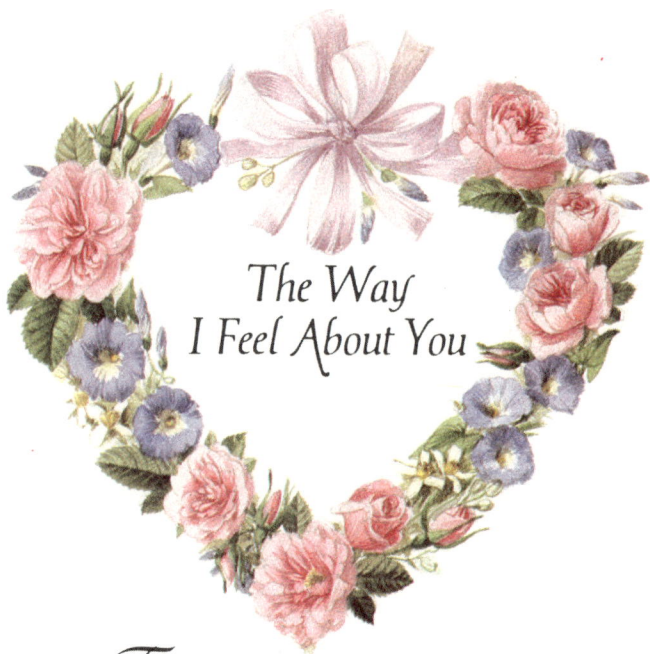

The Way
I Feel About You

*There's something special
about your smile
that stays with me
during our in-between times,
and makes me stop what I'm doing
and think of you...*

There's something special
about your love
that carries me
through a hectic day,
just knowing you are there.

There's something special
about you
that makes every day
I'm with you
one more reason
to want to be with you forever.

I wanted to find
   the perfect words
to make you realize
   how much
I need you and love you,
   but words
continue to elude me.
What would they be?
   Something poetic,
   I'm sure, heartfelt
and out of the ordinary.
I'm afraid it's no use.
Every time I look at you,
the words come out the same...

...I love you.

You're My Everything

What did I ever do?
What did I ever think about?
What did I ever feel
before there was you?

I can hardly remember
me without you,
and I'll never be the same again—
because there is you.

You are my yesterdays, todays,
and my tomorrows,
my thoughts and my dreams,
my hopes and my plans,
because you are my love.

*In the quiet times,
when I'm alone,
away from all the confusion
that is my day-to-day life,
I think of you.
When I can't be with you,
I like to think about
how much you mean to me,
how much our sharing
has enriched my life.
And when my quiet time has ended,
I can return to the everyday
renewed...*

*I find strength
and purpose
in my thoughts of you.*

For You,
My Love

I would give you the world if I could.
Instead, I will give you
all that is mine to give —
my hopes, my dreams,
and my love...
always my love.